Terminal Inferno

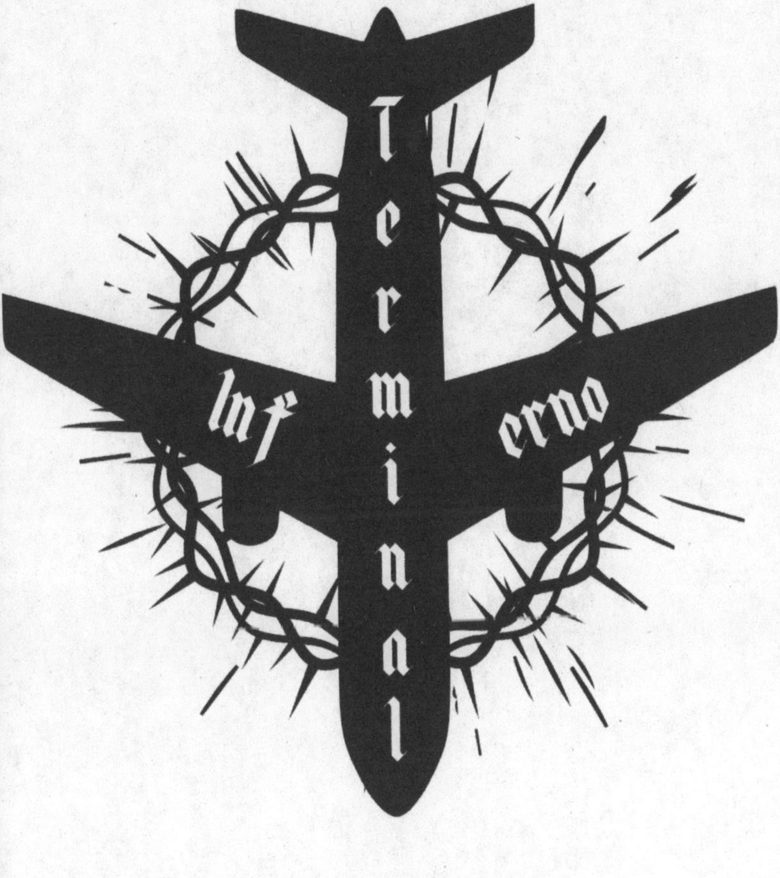

M.C. Crane

Terminal Inferno

A Novella

M.C. Crane

THE LAUGHING MAN HOUSE PUBLISHING

This book is a work of fiction. References to real people, events, establishments, organizations, or locales are intended only to provide a sense of authenticity, and are used to advance the fictional narrative. All other characters, and all incidents and dialogue, are drawn from the author's imagination and are not to be construed as real.

TERMINAL INFERNO

M.C. CRANE

Terminal Inferno

Praise for Terminal Inferno

"A eucharist of blood, lust, sorrow, and redemption, M.C. Crane's *Terminal Inferno* is a fever dream that demands witness and bares its soul on the pulpit for all to see. A gut-wrenching tale of what it means to love oneself and the power to that can be found within."

-Grace R. Reynolds, Elgin Award Nominated author of *The Lies We Weave*

"Terminal Inferno is a fast and furious gut punch that is sure to gift countless queer readers a powerful sense of kinship and much needed catharsis. It's left me eager to read more from M.C. Crane!"

-Lennox Rex, author of *I'll Never Leave You: Stories*

"I've never read a book that so viscerally understood how it feels to be queer, trans, and disabled. From the pain of well-meaning hatred and ignorance to the wince inducing betrayals of the body. M.C. Crane has found a way to encapsulate what it's like to be in the innermost hell of the soul and how hard it is to break the cycle of self hatred and insecurity. Sometimes the real nightmare isn't the ones in your mind but the everyday situations you have to survive and the high cost it takes to be yourself. Several times I found myself putting the book down and yelling, "This is it, this is how it feels!" I'm definitely looking forward to whatever else Crane is cooking up."

-Olivier Way

"M.C. Crane's debut novella, Terminal Inferno, flays
queer religious trauma wide open. Demetrius's
warped sense of self and yearning for absolution feel
achingly familiar. Brokenness becomes his identity,
his shield: if he's already in pieces, there's nothing
more to shatter...until he's trapped with his own
psyche and nowhere to run. I hope this incredible
piece haunts my dreams."

-Shrike

Chapter One

"For fuck's sake!" Demetrius turned the corner into his terminal just in time to see the plane slowly backing away. He sucked in a breath, trying to calm his racing heart after running halfway across the airport.

More like aggressive limping, he thought to himself. Demetrius had never missed a flight before and he rubbed his temples, surveying mostly empty gates. At the far corner, he spied the customer's desk, a line already forming. Seems he wasn't the only one missing his flight. Once more throwing his worn black satchel over his shoulder, he hobbled over and got in line. He soon realized it would be a minute as they worked through the angry travelers ahead of him.

Awesome. We love standing in lines. To pass the time, Demetrius decided to text his sister.

I missed my flight.

Damn, Demi, really???

Yeah. I thought maybe I would make it if I ran but our landing was so delayed and this airport is fucking huge. We sat on the tarmac for like twenty minutes, swear to god.

I'm sorry dude. That totally sucks.
What are they gonna do now?
New flight?

Idk. Waiting in line. Lots of angry people here.

Keep me updated. And lay low, okay?

2

Terminal Inferno

That city isn't exactly 'friendly'.

Demetrius sighed and closed his eyes, pain shooting through both of his legs. He'd give anything to have a cane right now. He wished he hadn't been so reluctant to get one in the first place. It had really just been pride. He had felt too young to give in, but now the discomfort that had made a home in his lower spine had migrated. Over the last year and a half, the pain and swelling took over his knees and ankles and hips, while his sciatic nerve screamed from being pinched by an unrelenting disc. As if to put a point on it, his shoulders began to throb. He hunched over to compensate, suddenly feeling closer to eighty-four than thirty-three.

"Can I help the next person in line?" Demetrius opened his eyes, realized it was finally his turn and fumbled with his ticket as he approached the desk.

"Hi, my plane was delayed on the way in and it made me miss my connecting flight home. I've never had this happen before, what do I do?"

Behind the counter, a tall woman with long black curls and a tired complexion typed away on a worn-out keyboard. "Let me find you in the system."

"Okay," Demetrius shifted uncomfortably as the man behind him grew increasingly loud in his dissatisfaction of wait times.

"Where were you going?"

"Raleigh."

"Last name?"

"Delwood."

"First name Rebecca?"

Demetrius grit his teeth. "Yeah."

"I see. Well Ms. Delwood, we don't have another flight to Raleigh until 11:30 tomorrow night."

"Tomorrow night?! It's already nearly–" Demetrius checked his phone. "It's almost one am now, what do I do? Do you have vouchers for things like this? My sister mentioned it happened to a friend of hers–"

"Unfortunately, your plane was delayed because of the weather and we don't compensate for acts of God."

"Of course you don't."

Terminal Inferno

The woman continued, unphased, and handed Demetrius a pamphlet with a QR code. "You can scan this and get a discounted rate at a hotel for the night. I've gone ahead and put you on the plane for tomorrow night. Give me one second to print it."

Demetrius took the pamphlet in his shaking hands, desperately holding back the well of tears rapidly filling behind his eyes. He was already so tired. It had been a long day of connecting flights, lost luggage, and back pain. Now he was stranded in a strange city, a dangerous city, for nearly twenty-four hours.

After getting his ticket, Demetrius settled into an empty chair at the nearest closed gate and scanned the QR code. If he was going to be stuck, maybe he could at least be somewhat comfortable. His hopes disintegrated as he viewed the prices. They were all well out of his price range, even the ones a little further out thanks to the nearly eighty-dollar Uber fee.

Well I am stuck here til 11:30 tomorrow night :/

What???? There are no sooner flights???

Nope

M.C. Crane

That's fucking bullshit.

                    I know. I am already so tired.

Did they give you a voucher at least?
Like for a hotel?

                No, they said the airline doesn't cover
                     acts of god. It's giving homophobic.

Yeah well god is homophobic.
Christ.

                   They gave me a pamphlet with hotels
                          But they are all too expensive.

I can send you the money, I don't mind.

                   I know you would. Not sure I want to
                           leave the airport anyway.

That's so valid. Long time to wait tho.

                    Yeah. I guess I always wondered what it
                    would be like but I'm not into it now that
                    it's happening. Whatever. It's an adventure
                                                      ig

Terminal Inferno

Want me to stay up with you?

> Nah you work tomorrow. Ima hobble around and see if I can find a chill spot to hunker down. Try to sleep a little.

Aight. Solid plan considering. Don't get murdered tho, that would be really inconvenient.

> Wouldn't want to inconvenience you in any way. I'll try to stay alive and reflect on why this is happening to me.

Jesus is punishing you for your lifestyle <3

Demetrius laughed to himself. His sister, Julie, had always been there for him. She'd even helped him pick out his name and stood by him when he finally came out to their parents. Like good, god-fearing Christians, Demetrius' parents rejected him. They refused to use his preferred pronouns and continued to deadname him. It didn't take long for Demetrius to move out and in with his older sister and shortly thereafter, they both went No Contact with their parents. Demetrius had made peace with it–or as close to peace as he could get. The nagging fears of eternal damnation snuck up on him during the wee hours of the night, presenting as nightmares and shadows. Deep down, he still wrestled with the conflict of self and on more than one occasion had drafted an email to his mother which he never sent.

Demetrius surveyed the gates, the lines of people boarding the last plane of the night, the custodians sweeping floors and emptying trash, the customer service people chatting and changing shifts. Maybe it wouldn't be so bad. He checked the gate on his ticket and groaned. A35. He was all the way in D27. He would have to walk to a completely different terminal on the other side of the airport. Excellent.

He sighed and stretched, his back cramping from the movement. *Will not be walking tonight though, not like I don't have plenty of time to kill.* He thought about staying at his current gate for the night. It was completely empty, and the departure screens had no pending flights listed on their displays. The chairs were not the most comfortable, but he didn't expect to find any different and it was already so late. *Nearly three in the morning,* as he checked his phone.

As he settled into his chair, shifting uncomfortably, his eyes landed on a dark figure he hadn't noticed before. Demetrius rubbed his bleary eyes, and the shadow focused into a man. He sat primly, hands folded in his lap, feet tucked together flat on the floor, decked in a black suit with a white collar at his throat declaring his priesthood. *Catholic–maybe Methodist.* Demetrius shrugged. It was all the same to him. Religions blended together, each one colored in a different genre of hate. The priest's eyes were closed, mouth muttering in what Demetrius assumed was prayer. His eyes fluttered open and locked with Demetrius from across the room.

Demetrius immediately looked away and shuffled once more. He closed his eyes for several minutes, searching for a sleep of some kind but it hadn't shown up quite yet. Looking up through his eyelashes, Demetrius glanced towards the priest and was discomforted by the fact that the priest was still watching him.

Demetrius was used to people staring at him. It came with the territory. People assessed him constantly. Boy? Girl? Some mystery flavor in between? Demetrius was a puzzle even unto himself, let alone the world around him. The scrutinizing eyes became an adornment he wore as willingly as his smile. It was a pain to exist, but he would pretend not to notice. He was used to being stared at, but the determined gaze from the priest pulled at Demetrius and his religious upbringing. On a night of unpredictable discomforts, a priest was not a welcome sight.

Demetrius' head sagged against his palm. He was so very, very tired. He blinked in rapid succession, feeling the weight of the day come down and envelope him. He gave one more glance towards the priest who was now gone. Demetrius felt relieved and succumbed to the depths of his dreams.

Chapter Two

"**C**an you believe we are up this high?!" Demetrius blinked awake, sitting upright in his chair, a seat belt digging uncomfortably into his stomach. Through a sleep induced haze, Demetrius realized he was on a plane. *What the fuck?*

He rubbed his eyes and tried to stretch his back, which spasmed in silent agony. His right leg had gone numb and he stretched it down the aisleway, hoping to massage back some feeling.

Only then did he look around, startled to find that the plane was empty. The silence of it came crashing down as a suspicious panic took hold of his heart. There was no one ahead–Demetrius strained his aching neck–no one behind except–

In the last seat at the back of the plane sat the priest Demetrius had seen earlier. And he was still staring. The goosebumps prickled on Demetrius' arms, spreading up his back to his neck, a cold sweat overtaking him. Something was wrong. Surely, he hadn't slept through an entire day?

"Look, we can see the sun."

A voice next to him stirred Demetrius and he looked over to find a little girl with long, dark hair neatly arranged in two braids. Her back was to him as she gazed out the window.

"Do you mean the moon?" Demetrius asked, confused. "This is a night flight."

"No silly, it's the sun!" the little girl turned and looked up at him. "Don't you recognize it?"

Demetrius froze. His lungs constricted, his panic mounted, his heart beat so fast he felt he would faint.

A face of familiarity gazed at him, a face he had tried desperately to disguise and forget. He had stuffed her away so far into him it almost felt like she no longer existed. *Almost*. No matter how many pictures he burned, or how many times he shaved his head, she was there in every reflection. In the soft curve of his chin. In the shining topaz of his eyes. And now she was here, in the airplane seat next to him staring him down. He couldn't push her away now, even as he shrunk away from her. A despondent grief came over him, threatening to shatter his porcelain heart. Tears trembled along his lash line as he took in the floral dress and open face. A face that had always wanted to be seen and loved. She sat, waiting, finally refracted in his reflection and Demetrius could not look away. He expected her to scream at him, to blame him, to ask why he had abandoned her. Instead, she took his hand into hers and grasped it lovingly.

"We are flying towards the sun. It's okay."

The contact and emotion were too much. Demetrius swung his head around, unclasping his seatbelt and leaping from his chair. The sudden movement shot pain through his spine and he crumpled against the aisle seats. His head hung low as he tried to breathe through waves of fear and nausea. He tried fixating on the pattern of the carpet–an ugly pale blue with darker blue spots. His concentration was interrupted by a pair of black loafers and an overpowering aroma of burning myrrh.

The priest stood in front of Demetrius, grabbing a fistful of his short curls, bringing his head to eye level. With his other hand, the priest raised his fingers to his mouth in a shushing motion. He smiled, displaying sharp, pointed blackened teeth behind plump rosy lips. The plane began to rock violently as thunder echoed in the distance, jostling Demetrius who was still held firmly by his hair. He had no choice but to grab onto the priest for stability, and his hands were met with fire and burning. Demetrius screamed, letting go as the plane jerked to the left, his neck snapping under the grip of the demon priest.

Demetrius gasped, sitting forward, grasping his black T-shirt just above his heart. He panted and took in his surroundings. He was not on a plane and there was no small girl who shared his face. There was only the quiet hum of a nearly empty airport and whispered chatterings of other waiting passengers. Demetrius strained in his seat; his whole body wracked with pain. He flicked his phone screen to check the time, hoping a decent amount had passed. The phone blinked 4:37 am. *Damn. Basically nothing.*

"Excuse me."

Demetrius startled at a voice so close to him. He looked over and immediately paled as the priest lingered in the seat next to him. He wondered how the priest had snuck up, maybe it was when he had been sleeping? Demetrius had impeccable hypervigilance born from a childhood of hiding tripps and graphic tees, drawings of naked women, and diaries riddled with tried-on names and personalities.

Demetrius cleared his throat, "Can I help you?"

"You cried out in your sleep, I thought maybe you were having a nightmare," The priest's pale blue eyes bore into him, questioning and intrusive.

"Just a bit stiff and sore. Been a long day." Demetrius shrank back as far as he could in his seat.

The priest's gaze remained fixed. "Can I pray with you...?"

"Demetrius. And thank you but no, I'm good." Demetrius stood up, his satchel falling against his back.

"The Lord hears you even if you don't hear him."

"Yes, well, with all due respect, the Lord stopped recognizing my voice a long time ago."

The priest tilted his head. "I'll pray for you."

Demetrius gathered himself and began walking away. "I'd rather you didn't," he mumbled.

He looked back only once, the priest still sitting in the same spot, his hands folded in silent prayer. Demetrius frowned and rounded the corner, following the arrows to the C gates. He figured a little distance between himself and the priest couldn't hurt. He was certain the man meant no harm, but the encounter post nightmare left Demetrius feeling jittery. He swallowed anxiously and realized his mouth was dry. Stopping in front of a vending machine, Demetrius debated between hydration and comfort and opted for comfort via a nice cold Dr. Pepper. As the machine dispensed his drink, he opened the messages to his sister.

> Ran into a creepy ass priest. That was fun. I know you're asleep so I'll tell you tomorrow when you wake up. Also had a nightmarish dream. Maybe planes aren't for me.
> Love you.

Demetrius continued on his way, chugging his bubbly drink that awakened his tired senses. He passed more people through the concourse. Some were sleeping, stretched across the floor, tucked against the wall. Demetrius wondered if they were displaced as he was. He briefly considered laying on the floor himself but quickly discarded it at the thought of having to get back up. As he came up to the C gates he checked his phone again, coming up on five am and a 15% battery life. He needed to find a seat and a charge port quickly. But first, a little more distance.

Demetrius finally settled himself on C18, a flight leaving at 6:30 for Chicago. There were a few souls there already, tired faces dissociating into phones and books and eyelids. As he made his way to a far seat near a wall outlet, he was relieved to see that no one sported a distinct white collar. As he eased himself toward the seat, his knee gave out, causing him to fall, smashing the back of his thigh into an armrest.

"Fuck!"

Demetrius hissed as he lowered himself onto the seat. *That is definitely going to bruise.*

He quickly looked around, but no one seemed to have noticed his disruption. He was glad. No more unwanted conversations with strangers. He adjusted the seat, unable to find a position that alleviated the pain in his lower back and hips. Dipping into his satchel, he pulled out his phone charger and a bag of various medications.

Demetrius kept a miniature pharmacy with him whenever he traveled, prepared for any outcome or side effect. Muscle relaxers, Tylenol, ibuprofen, lidocaine patches, a prescription of Zofran for nausea because of the muscle relaxers, Colace for constipation because of the muscle relaxers, and melatonin for when the pain kept him awake. He rolled the muscle relaxers in his hands, debating. He ached all over so badly, but he knew the relaxers would make him groggy. He had plenty of time to sleep it off, and maybe actually get some sleep. Still, he was in a strange airport in a strange city, surrounded by strange people. His back spasmed again and, against his better judgment, Demetrius swallowed the round, orange pill and washed it down with a swig of his sweating bottle of Dr. Pepper. It wouldn't take long for the pill to kick in.

Around him, new future passengers shuttled into the gate. He checked his phone battery, contemplating leaving but it registered only at 30%. He needed a bit longer and he worried that if he left his spot, he may not find another one so conveniently close to a charge port. He felt a little guilty for taking up space and hoped he was tucked far enough away that his presence ultimately wouldn't matter. Nobody was looking at him anyway. Everyone was caught up in their own world. Who wants to be at an airport at 5:30 in the morning?

Not me. Demetrius rubbed his bare arms wishing for a sweater or a hoodie. No such luck as his luggage was miles away in another state. He started to feel the relaxers kick in as a warm sensation overtook him. It started in his legs and worked its way up until his whole body felt light and fuzzy. He closed his eyes, savoring the feeling of becoming mush. Around him, the noise picked up as more people arrived, but it was filtered through exhaustion and drugs. In a matter of moments, Demetrius' chin fell into his chest and his even breathing welcomed him to the land of sleep.

lames licked Demetrius' fingers as he stood before a white pillar candle. He blinked, confused, shaking the lit match he was holding. Before him was a small wooden table, covered in a white and green altar cloth, in the center of which was the candle in a silver cup. Behind the altar, elevated on a stage, stood a tall oak pulpit with a matching cloth emblazoned by a golden cross. Demetrius stepped backward, bumping into the pews behind him. He turned to find himself in an empty church. But not just any church. *His* church.

The pristine white walls interrupted by colorful stained-glass windows threw Demetrius' heart into a panic. He clutched his chest, feeling the erratic beating of his heart through his shirt. He tried to breathe evenly, but each inhale felt more suffocating than the last. He didn't know how he got here, and he didn't care–he needed to get out, now.

Demetrius staggered down the path between the pews heading for the back of the church. His movements were stilted and slow, as though his flesh had been replaced by a soft rubber. He kept his gaze fixed on the doors, but each time he blinked they seemed further away. After what felt like an eternity, Demetrius looked back, thinking surely, he had come a far way. Instead, the altar loomed directly behind him, a silver goblet and tray now on either side of the candle.

The room began to swirl and shift, growing darker. The air was thick with burning myrrh which made it even harder to breathe. Demetrius fell to his hands and knees in front of the altar, his heart beating so fast he was sure it would burst. He didn't understand what was happening, but he was too weak to do anything but try and survive. Demetrius turned and began his crawl back down the aisle as the lights continued to dim. Darker and darker, he crawled across a red worn-out rug until finally the last of the light disappeared and Demetrius was plunged into darkness.

Before his panic could heighten anymore, Demetrius heard the flick of a match and he looked up, coming face to face with the edge of the altar and a pale white hand reaching down from the pulpit to light the candle. The candle illuminated just enough so that Demetrius could see the goblet and tray covered in little round wafers. He tried to pull himself up, but the movement was futile. His knees stung and ached, but he felt if he tried to move, he would only collapse.

A soft hand pushed through Demetrius' curls, gripping them firmly before releasing and caressing his face. The touch was cold, sending a shiver down his spine. The hand seemed to sense it, following it, trailing two thin fingers down his back, stopping just above the waist of his pants. Grunting, Demetrius pulled his head up and over, only to see the priest of nightmares sitting in the pew beside him.

"Rebecca," the priest murmured.

"That's-not-my...name," Demetrius huffed between labored breaths.

The priest sighed. "Demetrius. What a name you chose for yourself. *Earth-lover*." he shifted in his seat, placing a palm on Demetrius' lower back. Beginning gently, he massaged in small circles from left to right.

Demetrius moaned from the touch, the ice-cold hand drawing out the inflammation that burned within him. It was the first relief he had felt in days. His head continued to swim, unable to hold a cohesive thought. He tried to remember when he came into the church to begin with, but each time the priests' hand would disrupt his thoughts. He tried to remember leaving the airport, coming back to his hometown, to this church. A place he had vowed to never return.

"You left without taking communion," the priest whispered, his hand snaking up Demetrius' back and into his curls. He took a handful, scraping his nails against Demetrius' scalp as he formed a fist. The priest pulled Demetrius' head upwards, reaching for the wafers with the other.

"The body of Christ," he whispered reverently, bringing it to Demetrius' lips.

Demetrius kept his mouth shut, his jaw trembling. Tears began to form in his eyes before slowly dripping down his cheeks.

"Open your mouth and receive the body of Christ," the priest urged.

Demetrius shook his head weakly as more tears spilled. His whole body was beginning to tremble from the pain of being on his hands and knees. The ache in his back had spread and every place the priest had touched now burned as if on fire.

The priest surveyed Demetrius, frowning as Demetrius glared at him in anger and disgust. He leaned forward slowly, 'til he was close enough for Demetrius to feel the coldness radiate from his skin. He cocked his head to the side, keeping eye contact with Demetrius and slowly opened his mouth, parting his sharp, blackened teeth, and extended a long, purple tongue. Demetrius tried to pull back, but he was held firmly in place by the priest's grip in his hair. The tongue snaked towards him, 'til it landed on his right cheek, catching a wayward tear. The tongue dragged upwards, following the trail to Demetrius' eye where it stopped and probed along the lash line. Demetrius could only watch in horror as the purple tongue withdrew, the priest closing his eyes and savoring the flavor of Demetrius' pain and confusion. The tongue snaked out again, faster this time, catching all of Demetrius' tears hungrily, sloppily, as the priest licked up Demetrius' face. He moaned around each one, closing his eyes, his free hand still prodding the wafer into Demetrius' pursed mouth. Demetrius attempted to calm his tears, but they only fell more violently after each contact with the priest's tongue. It seared his skin, as if it were a branding rod. Demetrius imagined his face covered in cross shaped burns and retched at the thought.

The priest took the opportunity to force the wafer into Demetrius' mouth, holding his hand across the lips to prevent Demetrius from spitting it out.

"Take this body of Christ," he said, purple tongue withdrawn.

Demetrius gagged around the wafer. It tasted salty and bitter and clung to the insides of his cheeks. He was too dehydrated to swallow so instead he just choked.

The priest raised the goblet next. "The blood of Christ, shed for you." He tipped it towards Demetrius' mouth and this time Demetrius did not fight him. He sucked down the offering thirstily, but it was not quenching. Instead, it was thick and warm and tasted as salty and bitter as the wafer. Demetrius forced himself to swallow, his stomach threatening to expel the contents.

"What a good boy," the priest commended. "I knew you could obey. Again."

To Demetrius' horror, the priest raised a second wafer to his mouth and pushed it past Demetrius' chapped lips. Demetrius had no choice but to chew and attempt to swallow. The priest massaged Demetrius' neck before raising the goblet.

"The blood of Christ, shed for you."

Once more the thick, salty fluid ran down Demetrius' throat. He gagged and began to cough but the priest snatched his face, forcing his lips shut.

"Good boys who wish to be forgiven do not spit."

Demetrius swallowed again, the bitterness coating his tongue. He closed his eyes, expecting it to be over but was again met by another wafer. He repeated his suffering, gagging and choking.

Surely that goblet has to be empty, he thought.

As if in response, the priest raised it to Demetrius once again.

"For thus says the LORD God of Israel: 'The bin of flour shall not be used up, nor shall the jar of oil run dry.'"

Over and over, the priest filled Demetrius' mouth, and each time Demetrius choked and gagged down the holy sacrament. Over and over and over until his stomach began to expand and grow, straining against his waistband. The tears continued to fall, licked and savored by a flaming purple tongue until Demetrius collapsed completely on the floor, his head still held upright by his hair. Demetrius consumed wafers and wine until there was no room left, and the communion dripped from his mouth and down his chin. He was exhausted and did not know how he would ever escape this.

"You had so many communions to make up for," the priest spoke, finally letting go of Demetrius' hair, letting his head fall to the floor. Demetrius cried at the impact and strained to move his crippled body. His stomach felt close to bursting and the offering around his mouth had grown cold, leaving a film on his lips and throat.

"Do you remember your first communion?" the priest asked, running his fingers through Demetrius' curls.

Demetrius nodded, silently.

"Do you remember your last?"

Demetrius didn't answer. He didn't move. He didn't acknowledge.

But of course, he did. He would never forget.

"No daughter of mine is giving into this trans propaganda!" the words hung in the air lost in the chasm steadily growing between Demetrius and his father. "We clearly gave you too many freedoms, trusted you far too much."

Demetrius took a step back, remembering the last time he had been too close, the handprint that had branded his face for a week.

"I don't know why it's such a surprise," he countered desperately, "You saw the signs you know you did! You can't keep denying it!"

"I'll tell you what I saw," replied his father. "I saw a rebellious, devil-filled child who enjoyed making her momma and I suffer," he threw his hands up to the ceiling before slamming a fist on the table. Demetrius jumped.

"I don't know what I did for God to punish me with a child like you but it surely must have been terrible."

Tears welled in Demetrius' eyes, spilling over and staining his cheeks. He turned to his mother and pleaded with her.

"Momma this is who I am, this is how God made me. You used to tell me I am fearfully and wonderfully made. Why do you only see the fearfully part?"

Demetrius' mother stood behind her husband, silently crying, clutching her well-worn bible. She mirrored Demetrius in every way–tall, fair, with black curly hair and Demetrius hated that they shared so much. She did not answer him and continued to quietly sob.

"It wasn't enough when you stopped wearing dresses, when you didn't wear the jewelry people bought for you out of the kindness of their heart. It wasn't enough when we confiscated your...your pornography, hell I could have forgiven that if it had least been *men*." His father continued, on fire for his God. "It wasn't enough when you went and cut off your beautiful hair. Now I know I was angry and I shouldn't have reacted that way but the devil in you has tested me to my limits."

Demetrius interrupted, "It wasn't pornography it was drawings of the female form–"

"Naked. Women." his father interjected. "Call it what you like but at the end of the day a spade is a spade. It's pornographic. And you know what God thinks of gay people, we taught you all about Soddom and Gomorrah on that day. In fact every day since then we've been patient and prayerful with you. We've read scriptures over you, signed you up for every bible study there was–we've done everything to show you the mercy of God."

"You've done nothing but show me the hatred of God!" Demetrius screamed back, balling his fists.

In one stride, his father was on the other side of the table and in front of Demetrius. He grabbed him by the little hair he had left and dragged him through the living room and down the hall before throwing Demetrius into his room.

"I don't want to see or hear you until I call for you," his father screamed, pointing an angry finger in Demetrius' face. He straightened up and looked at his child coldly. "You are such a disappointment. You and your sister. But you–I had hope for you. I even picked out a suitor for you and let me tell you, that was all the Lord's doing because no good man would ever look at," he waved over Demetrius, "*this* and want it. No one is ever going to want you. You think you'll find freedom 'changing' your gender and cutting your hair? It's never gonna change who you are on the inside, *Rebecca*."

His father had turned and slammed shut the door and Demetrius had curled himself into a ball and sobbed. It was one thing to believe these things about himself. It was another to hear them voiced aloud by someone that he loved. And he did love them, his parents. Even if they couldn't seem to love him back.

For hours, Demetrius heard yelling and slamming from the kitchen, his father worked up and raging, his mother quietly agreeing and subduing. After Demetrius had calmed his racing heart he texted Julie and told her what happened.

I'll come get you. Right now.

I'm afraid to leave mom

Mom can fend for herself. She always has.

I'm scared Julie. I really hoped it would be different. I thought I would be enough.

You are enough. It's them who aren't.

Things hadn't been so bad lately.

They do that. They lure you into a false sense of security.

I thought since they loved me it would be enough.

You're not Jesus, Demetrius. Don't
let them nail you to a cross.

Demetrius suddenly realized the house was quiet. He picked himself up from the floor and sat on the edge of the bed. His head was throbbing as he weighed his options. He had hoped to work and save up a little more before he had moved out but his parents had made that nearly impossible. They'd forced him to get a job at the church, where of course he had to wear dresses and act modest and demure. His pay was next to nothing. At first it had been enough but over time, the walls of the church became claustrophobic and the real Demetrius suffocated under the lace and florals. Perhaps it was time to cut his losses and leave.

A knock sounded at the door, breaking his thoughts. He wiped his runny nose on the sleeve of his shirt and looked up as his mom entered.

"Can I come in?" she asked softly.

Demetrius nodded.

She sat down next to him on the edge of the bed and leaned forward, her arms parallel to each other as her hands hung limply. Demetrius spotted a blooming bruise on her left forearm and he swallowed the nausea thinking it was caused by him. There was a long silence between them before she spoke.

"You know your father loves you," she began.

Demetrius knew. It was the same way she started after every melt down.

"We just...don't know what we did wrong," she continued.

"You didn't do anything wrong momma. This is just who I am."

She looked at him sadly, brushing a fallen curl off his forehead. "When you were born, you were the most beautiful baby. Your dad was upset he didn't get a son but I was so grateful you were alive and healthy."

Demetrius winced and pulled his head away.

"It was a tough pregnancy. The doctors said I shouldn't have carried anymore after Julie but we knew the Lord had other plans. We've always trusted Him and He's never failed us. Not even now Rebecca." she reached for Demetrius' hand and he did not pull away.

"Demetrius," he whispered.

"D..." the word died on her tongue. "Maybe we just need to start over. We need a new beginning."

"I don't know how that can even happen."

She paused. "Do you remember when we used to go out to eat as a family? We would have the best times. I don't know why we stopped."

Demetrius knew why. It stopped when he stopped dressing in skirts and blouses.

His mother stood up and extended a hand to him.

"Come to dinner with us. Let's be a family again."

The tiny, delicate sprout of hope that Demetrius had been nursing for so long grew just a little bit more in the car. His father had only nodded to him as they walked out the door but Demetrius would take it. He would take whatever he could get.

That tender bit of hope, the very last that Demetrius had been holding onto withered within a second when they turned down the road to his church. It turned brown with decay as they pulled into the church parking lot and began to rot as they guilt tripped him up the steps and into the sanctuary. And who should be waiting there but the priest.

"Rebecca," he said, ushering them all to the front pews. "I understand you're feeling confused and you're battling some inner demons. I think we all know you've been battling them for a long time but now you have reached a crossroads and the devil is coming to claim you."

Demetrius sat silently. His heart was already broken. There was nothing left to render.

"John 10:10 says, 'The thief comes only to steal and kill and destroy; I have come that they may have life, and have it to the full.' Rebecca, if you go down this path, if you insist on rejecting the Lord's inheritance, you *will* be met with condemnation. You *will* burn in hellfire for eternity. You will be cast out of the Lord's favor and you will never see your family again. Instead, you'll be tortured, ripped apart, gutted and fed to dogs and demons. Your parents don't want that. I do not want that. You cannot possibly tell me that you want that."

Demetrius still did not answer.

The priest continued. "Your silence is not surprising. You know in your heart that you have nothing to rebut. You know what you are doing is wrong–"

"It's evil!" his father interjected, standing up between Demetrius and the priest. "It's demented. Satanic. You've brought evil into our home by welcoming it into your heart!" The screaming flung wet, hot spittle which landed on Demetrius' cheek and he flinched. He looked up into his father's eyes and saw the hatred growing in intensity. He supposed his father was right–there was evil in their home. But not from him.

The priest placed a hand on his father's arm, quieting him. Demetrius' father backed down, the rage and disappointment still smoldering in his eyes.

"I think what we need is a fresh start," the priest said.

Demetrius flicked his sight to his mother who refused to make eye contact.

"We should renew ourselves in the Lord. Let us pray. Heavenly Father, we ask for your divine intervention in this grave hour. We ask you to intercede on behalf of Rebecca. Rebuke the devil in her and bring her into your light. Break her pride, her stubbornness, her disobedience, and mold them according to your plan. Help us, Father, as we help Rebecca. Amen."

Amens echoed from his parents as the priest turned to the altar behind him, unveiling the ingredients for communion. On a silver plate and in a silver goblet were thin, half stale wafers that stuck to the roof of the mouth and slightly soured, room temperature grape juice. The priest offered first to his father and then his mother.

"The body of Christ," the priest murmured, "the blood of Christ."

Finally he turned to Demetrius and offered him a wafer.

"Take this body of Christ."

Demetrius did not answer and stared at the priest defiantly.

"The body of Christ," the priest continued, losing patience.

"I don't want it," Demetrius grit out.

"The body of Christ compels you!" the priest shrieked.

The sudden outburst from the normally soft spoken priest made Demetrius laugh.

Demetrius' father stepped forward, grabbing Demetrius' jaw roughly, pinning his son's arm down with his own knee. "Grab his other arm!" he barked at his wife.

She did not hesitate and lowered herself next to her child, holding down his other arm. Demetrius started to panic, jerking violently against them. His heart rate increased and he could feel the skin on his face start to break beneath his father's nails.

"The body of Christ," the priest spoke, shoving a wafer towards Demetrius' mouth.

Demetrius did his best to push away, shaking his head back and forth. But his father was stronger and he wrenched Demetrius' head forward, squeezing on either side of his mouth, forcing open his jaw. The priest seized the opportunity and stuffed in the wafer. Demetrius tried to spit it out but his father clamped a hand across his mouth.

"The blood of Christ," the priest recited, tipping the purple juice into Demetrius' forced mouth.

This time Demetrius coughed, choking on the sacrament and spraying it across the priest's white robes. Demetrius' father let go in shock as his son gasped and gargled. Demetrius' face took on a crimson shade as he struggled to catch his breath. He decided to risk it and dashed out of the pew, stumbling down the aisle way until he burst out of the doors. He tumbled down into the grass and took his first cleansing breath.

There was no going back from this. If he was going to burn, so be it.

"You were baptized by water, were you not Demetrius?" the priest continued, shaking Demetrius from his memory.

Demetrius did not answer.

"You went by Rebecca then, of course." A wet, cold liquid suddenly splashed across Demetrius' body, startling him. "You haven't been rebaptized as Demetrius. Haven't sought forgiveness for rebuking your inheritance from the Lord."

More cold liquid sprayed across Demetrius and the pews, soaking him to the bone. It continued to rain down on him until the priest's loafers appeared by Demetrius' face. The collared man knelt down beside Demetrius, a tin bucket at his side. He paused thoughtfully, once more running his fingers through Demetrius' curls. "You had such beautiful hair."

The priest raised the bucket, dumping it across Demetrius' face, practically drowning him in the process. The scent stung Demetrius' nostrils and he panicked as he recognized the odor.

Beside him, the priest raised his hands to the heavens, lighting a match above them.

"I indeed baptize you with water; but one mightier than I cometh, the latchet of whose shoes I am not worthy to unloose: he shall baptize you with the Holy Ghost and with fire."

With that, the priest's hands parted, and the match fell between them, landing and lighting Demetrius and his church.

Demetrius watched helplessly as the flames surrounded him and began creeping ever closer. He was reminded of the last time he'd faced a fire and how close he had come back then to being consumed.

When Demetrius was about twelve, the church hosted an October community indoctrination event complete with an epic bonfire. The Harvest Festival was a thinly veiled attempt to keep children off the streets during Halloween and out of the clutches of the devil. The church event boasted a corn maze, hay rides, and testimonies over candied apples. The night ended with a giant bonfire stoked with dried apple wood from a neighboring orchard.

Demetrius had reluctantly participated in the day's events, yearning for freedom and candy and a costume that would have let him be a little more *him* and a little less *her.* His mother had dressed him in a collared floral dress trimmed in lace that scratched at his arms and throat. His knobby knees stuck out from the bottom as he anxiously twirled one of his braids.

He'd been mesmerized by the lapping waves of the fire. All of the children had been given handfuls of powder that when tossed into the flames, caused them to change color. He approached cautiously, throwing his handful in and watching the oranges and yellows change to lavenders and blues. There was something in that fire that called to him and he hadn't been able to look away. He'd heard of interactions with the Holy Ghost and had yearned for an experience of his own. He hungered for something or Someone to reach down and fix him, make his insides reflect on the outside, much like Jesus reflecting from his heart. Demetrius had stepped just a little too close, leaned in a little too desperately.

"Is that you?" he had whispered, shaking. "*God*?"

Behind him, the next boy in line grew impatient and he shoved Demetrius, intending to push him out of the way. Instead, Demetrius stumbled forward, into the flames. He had just barely been caught by his pastor, who grabbed hold of Demetrius' long braids, and was yanked backwards to safety just as his dress had caught fire. The adults doused him with a bucket of cold, hay drenched water and praised God that he hadn't been burned alive. When Demetrius looked back, the colored flames were gone and he felt foolish for believing that any God would have chosen to speak to him.

The boy who had pushed him had been sent over to apologize but instead he had looked down at Demetrius disdainfully and whispered, "That's where you're going someday. You're gonna burn in hellfire for eternity. Freak."

The acrid smoke had clung to his nostrils and it was all he could smell for days. His mother had patched his floral dress until there was no trace left of the 'unfortunate incident' as she called it. Demetrius had his fill of fire–and the God burning within it.

The familiar smell filled him again but this time there were no colored flames tempting an offer of God's mercy and deliverance–only His wrath and judgment. Demetrius choked on the sacraments leaking out of him, and found little clean air to inflate his lungs. He tried to stand but grew too dizzy and was forced back to his knees as he continued to wretch. He couldn't catch his breath, he couldn't calm his heart and the panic seized him–

I am going to die here.

I'm going to die in this fucking church.

Demetrius knew it was too late for him even if he could stand. The fire now completely engulfed him, blocking every exit and eating up the pews as if they were full of sinners.

"You're gonna burn in hellfire for eternity."

The memory echoed in the air and he turned his head and spied the priest standing at the back of the church, completely engulfed and completely unbothered by the growing firey furnace. He smiled at Demetrius sinisterly, black teeth pointed and glowing.

A burning sensation began grazing Demetrius' forearm. He looked down in horror as the hairs on his flesh burned away into nothing, shrinking away from the all-consuming destruction. He jerked away, which only forced him into the fire on his other side. His clothes caught the flames, finally baptizing him fully. He screamed as his skin began to melt from his bones, dropping in sizzling chunks. He felt his lips split open, blood pooling down his chin, teeth cracking from the heat and filling his mouth with splinters. He waited to die, hungered for it, but he lingered in between, burning up as an endless fuel.

He began to fuse with the floor, unable to separate himself from the body of his church. He looked to the priest, still standing silent.

"Please," he begged, "Please let me die. Please, I want to die. Please make it stop! Make it stop! Make it stop!"

In an instant, the priest was there, lying next to him, face to face.

"What's wrong Demetrius? Don't you like being on fire for God?"

Chapter Four

Demetrius awoke with a start, a burning sensation radiating down his right arm. He shot upright, clapping his arms over his body to smother the phantom flames. It took several moments before he realized he was sitting in a terminal and not actively becoming a flesh puddle on a church floor. His heart was racing rapidly and his shirt clung to him in a cold sweat. The panic of being swallowed whole by a roaring fire had felt too real. Too visceral. Too eternal.

Terminal Inferno

He blinked wearily, cautiously, shaking free a trembling wrist that had been tucked and pinned underneath him. He coughed from tight lungs, an itch forming at the back of his throat as he took in his surroundings. He was still in gate C18, the flight to Chicago having come and gone as a new one was registered on the display. His phone had fallen between his thighs and was warm to the touch as he double tapped to check the time. It was 9:47 am and his screen was filled with missed text messages from his sister. He leaned forward in his chair and his stomach burned and gurgled. He couldn't remember the last time he had eaten. The wafers from his nightmare flashed in his mind but he pushed it away before the nausea could take him. He was still shaking, disturbed by the intensity of the dream, confused as to why here, why now. His heart had begun to calm, the burning and tingling in his arm fading as the blood circulated. *At least panic makes the blood pump faster,* he thought wryly.

Peeling his body from the black seat, Demetrius decided the next course of action was to find a bathroom. He felt gross from not showering and being in public so long and his body was stiff and sore. Apparently, the relaxers had done a good enough job to let him sleep awhile, even though it was not nearly enough.

Demetrius stood up too quickly and his heart palpitated. One of these days he was going to have to address that. He hobbled down the concourse, pain registering in his left sole. *Amazing.* As if the current pain wasn't bad enough, his sciatic decided to act up, pulsing down his leg all the way through his foot. It was agony to place his foot flat on the ground.

Pushing forward, he found a grouping of bathrooms, relieved to find a family one. He locked himself inside, before making his way to the mirror. He turned on the cold water and splashed his face before looking up. His eyes widened at the rosacea blossoming across his cheeks, meeting on the bridge of his nose. It was red and puffy, like a million tiny blood vessels had broken under his skin. He sighed and splashed some more water, hoping the coolness would calm down the inflammation on his face. It had been a while since his rosacea had flared up so prominently. Attributing it to the stress and mounting pain, Demetrius dabbed his face dry with a paper towel before erupting into a violent cough. He gasped and hacked, as if something was lodged deep in his chest. He coughed so hard, he spat into the sink, his mucus white and foamy.

Terminal Inferno

After wiping his mouth, Demetrius finished using the bathroom and decided that coffee was next on the agenda.

A little ways down, he found a little coffee place called Cool Beans. He snapped a photo to send to his sister. She enjoyed a good pun. After ordering a cold brew and blueberry muffin, Demetrius grabbed his sustenance and sat down at a nearby table. While he ate and sipped, he decided to catch up with his sister.

Creepy priests?? Of course you
would find the one priest there.
Dont some airports have like
chapels??? Dude you should look.

Also

Good morning! Now you just
have to get through the day
and you'll be home. The cats
miss you.

Ig I do too lolz

Text me when youre awake

Hey goodmorning

M.C. Crane

No chapels for me thanks.
They freak me out.

Had a rough night. Bad dreams.
But im fine now, I have coffee
so all my problems are solved.
Coffeeeee the solution
to all life problems brought
to you by homosexuals everywhere!

=P
Ha ha
Sorry you had a rough
night though. Hows your pain?

Meh

That good, huh? You should
check and see if they
have any sooner flights.

Well i think they would have
put me on one if there was.

Nah, sometimes theres like
connecting flights and

they put you on a waitlist.

Aight i'll check

Sick. Lemme know!

Demetrius sighed and cupped his head in his hands. He felt a headache coming on and preemptively took some Tylenol. He spied the bottle of relaxers and grimaced. After his dream, he wasn't sure if he'd ever be able to take them again.

That dream. For a brief moment, Demetrius revisited flashes of his memories intermingling with the horror from his imagination. It had felt too real, too painful. He flexed his legs, pointing out his toes and his knees cramped and twinged. He sat quietly, contemplating his existence when he looked up and spied the spectre haunting him. The priest.

The priest either didn't see Demetrius or was ignoring him. He walked past the crowded tables unhurried, his gaze pointed straight ahead. Occasionally he nodded to people passing him by. Demetrius kept waiting for the priest to turn his head and look at him. He steeled himself for the inevitable connection, almost willing the holy man to turn his gaze.

Goosebumps began to prickle along his skin as the priest continued past Demetrius' table unaware and without a passing glance. A cough disrupted his thoughts, and Demetrius suddenly became aware how crazy he was thinking. He had spoken to the priest all but once and it certainly wasn't the priest's fault he had been cast in Demetrius' hellfire slumbers.

Demetrius wasn't sure what compelled him to leave his chair and follow the priest. A morbid curiosity, maybe. Regardless, he threw his satchel over his shoulder and hobbled after the man of God. He kept a distance between them, at least three to four people. It felt safer, having a buffer. There was no shortage of people. The terminal was quickly filling with arriving passengers, the chatter and movement echoing off the tall walls and raised ceilings. Lines were formed at coffee shops and eateries, conversations were being shared, clumsy and oblivious people on cellphones were bumping into each other and clogging the passageway. The noise snuck up on Demetrius, piercing his eardrums and prodding into the headache that was steadily growing in the crown of his skull. He struggled to keep up with the flow of foot traffic, each hurried step forward causing a shooting pain in his foot and down his leg.

Terminal Inferno

At a merging intersection, Demetrius was forced to take a breather and lean against a wall. He kept his eyes fixated on the back of the priest but was interrupted by a group of people running from around the corner. One of them bumped into Demetrius, throwing him off balance, wrenching his left ankle.

"Oh my god, I'm so sorry," a short blond woman huffed as she backed up and continued. "My flight was delayed and I'm late, I'm so, so sorry." With an apologetic wave the blond ran down the concourse. Demetrius was perturbed at the interaction and irritated by the new tenderness in his ankle. On the same hand, he couldn't blame her. He knew all too well what it was like to run for your flight like a dog chasing a rabbit. He hoped she made it in time.

In the hubbub, Demetrius had lost sight of his priest. He was nowhere to be found. Demetrius rolled his eyes at himself. *What am I doing?* As luck would have it, he had paused not too far from the airline customer service and decided to check on his tickets. At least the line was shorter than last time.

When the next person was finally called, Demetrius was grateful to lean against the chest height crème-colored counter.

"How can I help you today?" asked a cheery man. His balding head and umber-colored skin was lightly coated in a veil of sweat. Now that he thought about it, it was a tad warm in this part of the airport.

Demetrius offered up his tickets. "I'm on a flight to Raleigh tonight but I was wondering if you had anything sooner."

"Okay one minute darlin', let me see what I can do for you." his fingers tapped rapidly across the keyboard, and he chattered vibrantly with his fellow employees. "Okay looks like there is a flight in about an hour leaving at noon across from us in C. Now it is a full flight so what you're gonna do is go over and find out if they have room for you when they start boarding."

"Oh, my God, thank you so much," Demetrius exclaimed. "I really want to get home; I got trapped here last night when I missed my original flight."

"Oh my word, how did you do that?"

"My first flight was delayed which caused it to overlap with my connecting one and I had less than ten minutes to run across the airport."

"What and you couldn't walk that fast?" the man joked as he printed out a new ticket. Demetrius might have laughed if he hadn't been so tired. He offered up a weak smile instead.

"Okay dear here's your new ticket, you just go right on over and check out what's happening."

"Thank you so much," Demetrius replied gratefully. Stacking the tickets up, he moved out of the way for the next customer.

"Hello darlin', how can I help you today?" the clerk's voice drifted after him and Demetrius smiled. It was nice to know that the clerk addressed everyone that way. That he was just nice. It made Demetrius feel warm and soft. And it made him miss his home. He turned back towards the C gates to C12 and stepped up to the airline service agent.

"Hi, I have a ticket for standby on this flight? They told me to come over here and see if there was room for me."

The agent took his ticket and scanned it into the computer.

"Yes, okay you are on the standby list, and it looks like there are two people ahead of you."

"Two people ahead of me?" Demetrius felt his hope and joy rapidly deflate.

"Yes, I'm so sorry. There are two people on standby ahead of you and it is a full flight, so for you to get on this flight, three people would have to not show up."

"Damn. So should I just wait over here then?"

The agent nodded. "Yes, just wait a bit and see if we have any no shows."

Demetrius crashed into an empty chair by the window. He couldn't believe his bad luck.

M.C. Crane

Flicking open his phone screen he decided to
share the misery.

> So they put me on standby for a flight
> That leaves in an hour.

Omg fuck yeah!

> Except

Oh god

> I'm third on the standby and its a
> full flight

FUCKKK

> Yeah. so three people have to not
> show up for me to get on this plane

This is ridiculous. You gonna wait to
see just in case??

> I mean, I think its pretty fuckin
> pointless but yeah ima wait and see

Well it's like eleven now so only
twelve more hours, worse case scenario

Terminal Inferno

Demetrius lingered in the gate, watching and envying the passengers boarding the departing plane. As the last one made their way down the tunnel, two people walked from the back of the gate to the service desk. No doubt these two were the other standbys. Everyone was anxious to get onto a plane and out of the airport. Demetrius didn't bother getting up from his seat. He figured if those people didn't get on, he certainly wasn't going to. Still, he waited and watched. The other standby passengers paced and checked their phones. It became clear pretty quickly that they would not be getting on the plane and the agents directed them back to customer service.

Demetrius sighed, annoyed at this thread of hope that had been so swiftly severed. He reconciled with himself that at least he had a ticket home, and a direct flight at that. Even if this one was delayed it wouldn't matter and there was nothing in the world to keep him from his flight.

A rumble from his stomach reminded Demetrius that food was a thing he should probably look into. He was nervous at the prospect of finding safe food that wouldn't agitate him and that wasn't going to cost him his left arm and a kidney. At least in an airport this large he was bound to find something, even if it was just another blueberry muffin. He hauled himself out from the seat and began his search, first by consulting a large map at the beginning of the C gates.

Splayed out from left to right, he could trace the whole path of the terminal and mini icons below showed food, bathrooms, charge areas, exits, and more. It was super convenient. Whatever direction he went in, Demetrius would find something. Just as he tore himself away to begin his hunt, his eyes glanced over a different type of icon: a kneeling person haloed by a cross.

A chapel. He realized he was headed in its direction, the same direction his priest had walked. Demetrius wrestled with himself for several minutes, irritated at even entertaining the idea of exploring it. After a bit of back and forth, he decided that it couldn't hurt to walk by. *One foot in front of the other*, he told himself.

It hadn't all been bad. If Demetrius was honest with himself, there were some things he missed about the church. He missed the sense of belonging, even if he had never truly felt like he had been a part of it. He missed the groupings of people dressed in their best, the plates of homemade cookies served with stale coffee, the children running between the pews and laughing because they were young and felt safe. He supposed he ought to be resentful of it, having spent most of his time on the outside looking in. He wanted to be resentful and truthfully, a part of him was—but there was still a lost, aching yearning that he couldn't quite shake.

Maybe it wasn't the church he really missed. Maybe it was just the sense of community. Maybe it was the hope of believing in a higher being, of being absolved from responsibility and individual purpose. The world was a lot bleaker when a person realized that they were in fact responsible for their actions and there was no divine power reaching down to guide and save them. The church and its people broke Demetrius. As he had changed and grown and stepped into his realization, he looked back to find that he had stepped alone. They mourned an identity they had never bothered to truly know and crucified the body that stood in the flesh before them. God only loved you as much as you reflected him and while they searched and scanned Demetrius, all they saw was Rebecca and a God that was as dead as she was.

The thoughts weighed heavily on Demetrius. He still wasn't sure why now of all times things were coming to the surface. He reckoned that it was linked to his new relationship with Jupiter, whom he was returning home from visiting. It was a long-distance relationship and the first openly queer one Demetrius had ever been in. Like him, Jupiter had his own brand of coming out trauma, electing to leave his old galaxy behind and create a new one. Demetrius admired the way Jupiter lived his life. He was brave and daring in ways Demetrius had only dreamed about, and he wondered every day why Jupiter chose to invest in him. Demetrius didn't believe in divine intervention but something about their first physical meeting was undeniably holy. It was the first time Demetrius had felt truly comfortable with himself outside of Julie. And it had terrified him.

His phone buzzed in his pocket, disturbing his reverie. Expecting a text from Julie, Demetrius instead discovered an alert from his flight app. *Your flight has been delayed.*

"You've got to be fucking kidding me." Demetrius opened the app and saw that his 11:30 flight home had been pushed back to midnight. *I guess that's not so bad. It's only half an hour.* It was just coming up on one pm and he was surprised they'd announced a delay that early. He looked over and up at the flight board and spied multiple yellow squares dotted across it. Apparently, lots of people were being delayed today. He guessed there was a comfort to be had in that.

Hey guess what? Flight outs

been delayed

No fucking way?! Do I
Need to just come get you??

Too far. And I'd never survive
the car trip home

Bahhhhhh fine i just wish
there was something I could do. Ooo oo
I could call and complain?!

You sound too hopeful so I'm
gonna say no

You never let me have any fun

Yes, I know

When you get back we are so
writing a strongly worded email

Does this strongly worded email
include a lot of fuck yous in it?

...probably

Warranted

Terminal Inferno

So i guess continue lurking in the airport, haunting the concourses?

Thats the plan. Gonna find some food

Ahh, travel scavenging

Demetrius paused for a moment before typing again.

They do have a chapel here btw

Good go beg jesus' forgiveness <3

The buzzing chaos of the crowded terminal was starting to get to Demetrius, threatening to turn his headache into a migraine. He pulled out his earbuds, thanking his past self for making sure they were fully charged. He popped them in and turned on his current favorite playlist, the music drowning out the world around him. It eased his anxiety quite a bit. Demetrius loved music. In another life he probably would have been a musician.

He decided to put all thoughts of the chapel out his mind and instead focus on something to eat. As he continued down the concourse, he entered a stretch of hallway of floor to ceiling windows. It was quite the view. Planes came and went, crew loaded flights and drove up and down the tarmac, and in the distance was a beautiful green forest framed by a clear blue sky. Demetrius could not help but stop and marvel at the sight, humming to his music quietly.

> *"Just running forward, a life like wires*
> *As I see the past on an empty ceiling*
> *I play along with the life signs anyway*
> *But hope to God you don't know this feeling*
> *Yet in reverse, you are all my symmetry*
> *A parallel I would lay my life on*
> *So if your wings won't find you Heaven*
> *I will bring it down like an ancient bygone"*

Demetrius watched as another plane rolled away from the airport and thought of Jupiter. He'd first met Jupiter online through a mutual Discord group. Over time, they found themselves talking more and more with each other in the chats until Jupiter finally DM'd Demetrius directly one day:

Thought maybe we could use our own space? :)

Demetrius answered back almost immediately and from then on it was basically nonstop texting. *Not that it had all been easy*, Demetrius sighed to himself. If there were runners and chasers in a relationship, Demetrius was the runner. As much as he admired and respected–even adored–how Jupiter lived his life, it refracted a light onto Demetrius. This light illuminated all the things Demetrius had neglected in himself, and all the things he had not yet healed. Demetrius struggled with his identity all the time, often feeling less than or that he didn't quite belong in the queer community. He was awkward and unsure and severely under experienced and all these things made him feel unworthy of Jupiter's time and affection. There was something about Jupiter that Demetrius couldn't explain but it was something he had never experienced before. If he had to describe it, Demetrius felt that being in Jupiter's presence was the closest thing to heaven he'd likely ever experience. When Jupiter cast his eyes on Demetrius and held his gaze, it was as if God himself was blessing Demetrius, bestowing him with loving favor. Demetrius could not help but love Jupiter, and love him he did– passionately and desperately. But also, terribly brokenly.

*"Do you remember me
When the rain gathers?
And do you still believe
That nothing else matters?"*

A single tear rolled down Demetrius' cheek and he quickly wiped it away. Being with Jupiter in person had been amazing. They'd had the best time, enjoying each other's company, stealing kisses, spending hot afternoons in cuddles and wicked pleasures. *And then I had to fuck it up,* Demetrius mourned. As much as he had tried, Demetrius' fear had gotten the better of him

"I just don't think I can do this," he'd said, dropping Jupiter's hand.

"What do you mean baby?" Jupiter responded, genuine concern shadowing his face.

"This…I, us…you. I just don't think I'm ready. It was too fast. Too soon." The panic had mounted, and Demetrius' heart palpitations had kicked in full force. "I'm sorry I just don't think it'll work out in the long run."

"Did I do something..?"

"What? No, it's not that. It's just, you have all this going on and I'm so far behind and figuring things out and if we keep going, you're going to figure out that I'm not who you think I am."

"Can we talk about this? I love you and I *do* see you. I know you have things to work out, we all do, and I want to be there with you through it. Just talk to me, please." Jupiter's pleading broke Demetrius' heart. He pulled back further, pushing towards the airport.

"There's nothing to talk about. Just, leave it be and go have a good life, okay? You deserve to be happy." and with that, Demetrius walked away, leaving his lover standing at the drop off and he didn't look back.

He hadn't heard from Jupiter since then and he didn't blame him. Demetrius had let his insecurities get the best of him and likely ruined the only good thing he had going. He opened his phone, navigating through his messages, opening the one with Jupiter. He clicked on the text box and stood silently while the text line blinked at him. What could he say? *I'm sorry, I'm an ass? Listen, I'm just super insecure because my parents didn't love me enough? You're basically like, my new god and I was never good enough for him either?* Demetrius closed his phone and groaned, leaning his head into the window. The coldness of the glass felt good against him, and he leaned there silently for a few more minutes.

*"The whites of your eyes
Turn black in the low light
In turning divine
We tangle endlessly..."*

A wave of nausea followed by another stomach rumble forced Demetrius away from the window and back on his walk. He wasn't going to solve any of his problems on an empty stomach dramatically staring out a window listening to angsty music. He smiled wryly to himself. If nothing else, at least the drama validated his gay.

As he meandered, taking in the sights he landed on a relatively quiet American fare dineresque place. It was in the B concourse which placed him closer to his gate and, most importantly, it had available tables and chairs. He placed his order, a simple cheeseburger and fries with a Dr. Pepper, and waited for his name to be called. To his relief, he didn't have to wait very long.

"Demetrius?" a young man with short brown hair called out.

"That's me."

"We're out of fountain Dr. Pepper but we just got some bottles in, so I gave you one of those."

Demetrius took his meal and sat down. The food wasn't spectacular. It was a little too salty and the soda was warm, but it still filled his stomach and quelled the rumblings. Meat wasn't his favorite option, but he knew he'd need the protein to make it through the rest of the day. He finished quickly, crumpling the greasy foil wrapper and stuffing into his fry holder. It settled like a lump in his stomach, and he hoped it wouldn't come back to haunt him. Disposing of the trash, he walked back into the hallway, deciding to continue his walk to the A gates.

Listening to his music and not quite paying attention, Demetrius turned around to get his bearings and realized he was just across from the airport chapel. Double glass doors were spread open wide with "Interfaith Chapel" written in bold, golden letters across the top of the entrance. A dark blue carpet welcomed in all people of faith, soft lights beaming from the ceiling. He walked a little bit closer and peered in, being careful not to step in. The walls were mostly bare and white, each one hosting a different solitary religious symbol. On the right side he saw prayer mats, in the center rows of pews, and at the left, groupings of plushy chairs. Demetrius couldn't deny that the padded chairs looked very comfortable. It was tempting–too tempting. His gaze wandered back up the aisle way between the pews and his stomach lurched when his eyes landed on a wooden table not unlike the altar in his dreams. This one, however, was bare.

He looked around and found the chapel to be completely empty. In a way, it felt less threatening since it hosted multiple faiths instead of just one. Demetrius took a breath and stepped inside. He took one earbud out and listened. It was surprisingly quieter here in the chapel and Demetrius suspected that they had insulated it somehow. *Wouldn't want to drown out the prayers of the sinners*, he thought ruefully. Relaxing a bit more since he didn't immediately burst into flames, Demetrius sank into the stuffed black chairs. To his delight, he realized it pushed back, and he could extend his legs and raise his feet. Stretching back, he finally had some relief. All the pressure points were cradled and the throbbing in his knees and ankles began to de-escalate. He put his earbud back in and closed his eyes. *I can finally dissociate in peace.*

The nagging fear of running back into the priest seemed a distant memory. Every so often Demetrius would open one eye and survey the room. Each time it was still empty, still quiet. Even if a lost soul had come wandering in, Demetrius was tucked into a far corner. He didn't think anyone would notice him and even if they did, Demetrius' vibe in general did not lend itself to easy conversation.

Intimidating. It was a word attached to Demetrius when he was still just a child. Even in pink dresses and blue bows, Demetrius had always been hard to approach. The boys called him bitchy; the girls called him unladylike. *Tomboy* had been used more than once but it went beyond that. There was a commanding presence to Demetrius, as if he was unbothered by anything and sure of everything. None of that was true, of course, but Demetrius leaned into the vibe. If he couldn't be what his parents or peers wanted, he'd be what they saw. The teenage years brought with them black eyeliner and ripped jeans, band tees and flannels, doc martens and a curly mullet with shaved sides. Black became his signature color. It only made sense to Demetrius, being the black sheep and all. He'd tried his best to be a good little lamb. He'd memorized the verses, worn the dresses, donned the braids and dead inside doe eyes. It seemed no amount of redeeming blood had been enough to save him. Each time he prayed and washed in the blood of Christ he came out blacker than before.

His parents had been tolerant up to a point. It was just a phase, they said. As long as Demetrius went to church in his pretty pink florals, everything else could be forgiven. More scriptures could be read and memorized; more prayer circles could be organized. The day that Demetrius cut off his hair was the day that every facade his parents carried had been shattered. His parents, particularly his father, had been so proud of the thick, luxurious hair Demetrius sported. It had spilled down his back in shiny ringlets, teasing the waistline of his clothes and the hearts of potential husbands.

"Your hair is your glory," his father had told him, "It's a gift for your future husband."

The thought of a man running his hands through his curls, pulling it into a sweaty fist while Demetrius was jackhammered dry on his wedding night had made his stomach burn. It was bad enough that he'd watched his father on more than one occasion grab his mother's hair to get her attention, to force her to her knees in prayer, or hold her under the water to purify her sins. The images of being yanked and forced lingered and only grew worse when he heard church boys making crude comments about dual braids. He wasn't going to let any of that happen to him. He'd made himself an appointment at a salon a few towns over and cried with joy when the stylist ran the razor above and behind his ear.

It was not the first time his mother had cried over him. It was the first time his father had hit him.

Demetrius felt his eyes grow heavy and the weariness of the last twenty-four hours crept up on him. He was afraid to fall asleep and dream again. It was cliche and Demetrius knew it, but the past he'd been outrunning seemed to be catching up with him. When his world had finally come crashing down around him in ruins, Demetrius took off and didn't look back. He jumped straight into the world, immersing himself in his culture, looking for new friends and romantic interests. He'd gotten close to and then broken up with a handful of people before he met Jupiter. Each time he had always gotten scared and ended things before it was too real. But then everything changed when he met Jupiter and for the first time in his whole life, Demetrius actually wanted to be better. He cared what Jupiter thought of him, and he knew that he would have to fix the holes in his own heart if he was ever to be happy. From Jupiter's brilliant, refracted light Demetrius saw himself, truly, for the first time. And it hurt. It burned. It ached. Demetrius desperately wanted to fix it but his fear of not being enough, of being too broken, of confronting those deep hurts was too much and just like before, Demetrius jumped ship.

He tried to shift his thoughts away from Jupiter, but he couldn't help himself. The warm summer afternoons tangled in moss-colored sheets listening to Jupiter's heartbeat had become Demetrius' safe space. The pain was too much, and the world was too loud, so his mind searched for peace and it landed on Jupiter. He pulled out his phone again, pulling up Jupiter's text chat and stared at the blinking text line again. He could only imagine how Jupiter must be feeling. Betrayed? Angry? Used? The last one threatened to undo the carefully constructed dam behind Demetrius' eyes and he clicked off the phone screen. He'd never meant to use anyone and especially not Jupiter. Had he?

He sank further into the chair and into his grief, replaying his past failed relationships. Had he just been using other people to validate his experience? Was he looking for some kind of recognition reflected back in the eyes of his lovers? Was he just as bad as the God he used to worship, demanding attention and reverence and throwing it away when it wasn't enough? Despite himself, the tears began to stream down his cheeks, building into uncontrollable sobs. The pain and grief wracked his body, doubling him over as he sat up. He didn't know what was wrong with him, what part of him was so broken that he couldn't accept love–or give it. And he wanted it, so desperately. He cried and cried, until his eyes were raw and his nose snotty. He was grateful for the tissues on the table beside him, balling them in his fist as he continued to weep. He blinked rapidly, trying to clear his eyes as he steadied his breathing. Remarkably, he felt better. Lighter. He ached, but it was a good ache. It was good to know that he could still feel things, even if it was painful.

He spent so much time locking his emotions away. He'd learned not to cry when he was a kid. He didn't cry when his mom confiscated his comfort clothes and music, he didn't cry when the priest at his church targeted him at a service and prayed for Demetrius to suffer so he'd turn to the Lord, he didn't even cry when his father had slapped him across the face after Demetrius had cut off his hair. Looking back, Demetrius reckoned the last time he'd cried was when at a book fair when he was about ten. His peers were circling the fair together and when Demetrius had tried to approach and join, the boys and girls redirected and spent the day actively avoiding him. The disdainful eye contact and pointed whispers stung and Demetrius had gone home early and cried in his room.

"Don't you think it's a little bit your fault?" his mother had said to him, wiping his tears with a wetted washcloth. "If you just tried to fit in and be more like those pretty girls, you'd have lots of friends. But it's like you don't even try."

After that, Demetrius never went to his mom for comfort or advice. In fact, he stopped talking to his parents altogether, beyond the obligatory conversation. He couldn't trust himself with anyone. Rejection was too hard, and Demetrius decided early on that he was better off in his own company, where he could be unruly and unorthodox and unwanted in silence. It was just easier to keep everyone at arm's length. Except Julie, of course. She didn't tolerate any bullshit from Demetrius.

"I'll always be honest with you as long as you are with me," she had told him. "I am on your side always and I don't give a fuck what our parents or the church or anybody has to say about you. You're my annoying little kid brother and you always have been."

Demetrius couldn't wait to get home. If he could get on that plane and land safely in his home state, then maybe he could work on fixing things in his life. Maybe, if he was incredibly lucky, he could even work things out with Jupiter. Demetrius doubted that he himself was worthwhile, but he had absolutely zero doubts that Jupiter was. Plus, he knew Julie would be pissed when she heard about their falling out, a fact he had conveniently neglected to tell her. From the beginning she had been a hard-core Jupiter fan and had done her best to foster their relationship. Demetrius wasn't sure where he'd be if it wasn't for Julie. *Probably be dead by now if I'm being honest.*

The crying had taken the final reserves of Demetrius' energy, and he leaned back into the recliner. He was grateful that no one had walked in during his meltdown and decided to set aside everything else for a much needed nap. He checked his phone which showed it was just a little past three. He set an alarm for 9pm, just as a precaution. He didn't think it was likely that he would sleep through his flight but he wasn't willing to risk it.

Chapter Six

emetrius shifted into the seat, stretching out and back. He marveled at the comfort but wasn't surprised by it. Churches always had expensive taste. Before he knew it, he was slipping back into his safe place, nestled in the arms of his beloved. It felt so real that Demetrius swore he could almost hear Jupiter breathing. In his mind, Demetrius nestled into Jupiter's chest, nestling himself between his boyfriend's breasts. He was as close to his soul as he could get without cracking open his ribcage and climbing inside. Demetrius lulled himself with the thoughts of Jupiter's soft skin, his fragrance, the way Jupiter's fingers liked to trace across Demetrius' throat and under his chin. He missed him so much. Too much.

Demetrius wasn't sure what it was that prompted him to open his eyes. It started as a creeping tingle on the back of his neck, as if each tiny hair was standing up one by one. The soft, golden visions of Jupiter became cloudy. He suddenly became acutely aware of his fingertips, each one suddenly achingly cold. With a shiver, Demetrius opened his eyes. The lights in the chapel had dimmed significantly, some even flickering creating a hazy, static atmosphere. The sound had disappeared as well. The hubbub of a bustling airport had quieted entirely. It was eerie. It was uncomfortable.

Demetrius blinked groggily, sitting up in his chair. The doors to the chapel were now closed, the terminal hallways shrouded in somber darkness. A panic set in and Demetrius picked up his phone to check the time, worrying he had somehow overslept and missed his flight. The screen was smudged, and he couldn't make out the time through his bleary sight. Rubbing his eyes, he looked around the room and froze when he reached the front pews.

In the front row of the pews lined up closest to him, sat a man dressed in black. His back was to Demetrius, but Demetrius knew exactly who it was. The priest. The breath in Demetrius' lungs evaporated as his panic mounted. He felt a cold sweat break out across his body, followed by a numbness in his chest and arms. He sat up quickly, the sudden movement sending a spike of pain down his back. He pushed through it, heading towards the chapel doors. He had to get out.

Before he reached them, a whispery voice slithered up the aisle way into Demetrius' ears.

"Demetrius. Have you come back for another communion?"

Demetrius ignored him and reached for the door handles. A swoosh of cold air ran through him followed by hot breath on the nape of his neck.

"Demetrius."

Demetrius whipped around expecting to see a demonic smile but there was no one there. He turned back but the doors were gone, and he was met by a blank white brick wall.

"Fuck!" Demetrius pushed into the wall, slamming his fists against it but it didn't budge.

His breath was fast and ragged, and he clutched his chest, feeling the erratic heartbeat beneath his skin. He couldn't afford to faint, not now, but he didn't know how to calm the panic and fear feeding his adrenaline rush. He closed his eyes and tried to even out his breathing.

"DEMETRIUS!"

An unfamiliar and unwelcome force compelled Demetrius to turn around and open his eyes. Down the aisle between the pews in front of the altar stood the priest. He was wearing long black robes now, the white collar around his throat practically glowing. His eyes glinted red and when he smiled, his forked crimson tongue peaked from behind the black razor teeth. If he had been hiding his true self before, it was now on full display. His coiffed golden hair and smooth skin belied his demonic appearance, seeding complicated feelings in Demetrius' chest. The priest was horrifying and beautiful and Demetrius hated himself for thinking so.

"Come to the altar, Demetrius."

Demetrius did as he was told, his senses suddenly dulled, his mind fuzzy and clouded. He staggered forward, almost drunkenly. The demon priest waited patiently for him, the determined, smug smile never leaving his face. Demetrius wanted to struggle, he wanted to fight against the force pulling him forward, but he was too tired and too confused. He reached the end of the pews and stood before the man of God. The priest reached his hand out, patting Demetrius' shoulder, ushering him down to the floor. Demetrius fell to his knees, his hands between his legs, his back slightly arched as he gazed upward.

Demonic eyes blazed down at him, a smile of black razors widening as the creature began rearranging his robes. Demetrius found himself face to face with tight blond curls shaped like an upside down cross, the tip of which pointed to a glistening slit.

"It's time to worship, Demetrius. Consider it my blessing to have chosen the form you prefer. Now offer unto the Lord your God your pretty pink tongue."

Demetrius opened his mouth, his tongue peaking between his lips. The demon reached towards him, wrapping his hand around the back of Demetrius' head, threading his fingers through the silky black curls. Spreading his legs, he pulled Demetrius into him, sliding the pointed tongue between two swollen lips.

"Worship," the priest commanded.

Demetrius began to lick. He closed his eyes and tried to think of anything besides what was happening. His thoughts twisted and he thought of Jupiter, of his smooth inner thighs, his warm vanilla scent, his sweet and salty taste.

Demetrius began to lick faster. His tongue explored the folds and dips, his lips hungrily sucking. The priest did not taste like Jupiter, but Demetrius looked for him anyway. He lapped at the entrance desperately before sinking his tongue deep inside.

The priest began rocking his hips, riding Demetrius' face. He twisted Demetrius' curls harder.

"The tongue is a fire, a world of evil," he panted. "The tongue is among the parts of the body, defiling the whole body and setting the course of nature on fire."

Demetrius picked up his speed, gripping onto the priest's legs for leverage. He bobbed his head, sucking and dipping alternating between the swollen clit and the wanting entrance. His face was hot and moist, and he could not tell the difference between the priest and his own tears. He dedicated himself to bringing the demon to climax, hoping that it all would end, and he could rest.

"Your mouth utters your iniquity, and you choose the tongue of the crafty." The priest picked up speed, grinding so hard into Demetrius' face he couldn't breathe. "Though evil is sweet in his mouth, and he hides it under his tongue."

With both his hands buried in Demetrius' curls, the unholy man of God finally came, erupting down Demetrius' throat and all over his face. The priest uttered a guttural growl, savoring the last waves of pleasure, pressing himself on Demetrius' lips.

Demetrius became still, feeling the warm pulses of the priest's orgasm against him. Lust and pheromones ruled him now and his legs shook from his own need. He didn't dare speak or move, afraid of any unexpected consequences. But he felt the sticky slickness between his own legs and in shame and confusion, he wished the priest would return the favor.

The priest stepped backwards from Demetrius, patting him on the head. "What a good little lamb you are," he whispered. He snapped his fingers and in an instant, Demetrius found himself prone and naked on all fours, on the stage of the church. He looked out over the pews still shrouded in darkness, becoming acutely aware of his position. A cold breeze prickled his skin, stimulating his nipples and drawing more attention to the growing wetness between his legs.

A beam of light clicked on above him, showcasing his naked form. He was grateful there was no one there to witness his certain destruction. He felt movement behind him, and two hands grabbed his hips roughly, raising them up and smashing his face into the floor.

"Therefore, I urge you, brothers and sisters, in view of God's mercy, to offer your bodies as a living sacrifice, holy and pleasing to God—this is your true and proper worship." The priest's voice echoed and bounced off the walls, booming as a service on fire.

With his ass and cunt on full display, Demetrius felt a tongue slide first across his cheeks and then in between them. He held his breath as it wriggled at an unforgiving entrance. It darted in and out, sparking gasps of surprise from Demetrius. A deep blush rolled over him as the demon continued to lick and prod him on the church stage. Moving lower, the priest cast his tongue to Demetrius' other entrance, this one eager and wanting. He circled, teasing, dragging down to the clit and sucking hard. Demetrius moaned and tried to pull from the desperate suction, but the demon kept him pressed into the floor.

While the devil's tongue continued to tease and plump his clit, Demetrius felt two fingers begin pushing inside him. Demetrius could not keep himself from leaning backwards onto them, his need overtaking his senses. He cried and moaned with abandon, desperate to come. The priest kept him right there on the edge, torturing him until it ached.

Without warning, the priest suddenly pulled away, and Demetrius cried out in frustration. The demon traced his fingers up Demetrius' back as he walked forward. Something hard struck Demetrius in the ribs, stealing his breath, and traced up his body until it hit just below his chin. There was just a slight pause before the priest circled in front of Demetrius, thrusting a bright red strap-on down his throat.

"Suck," the priest commanded.

Demetrius obeyed. He ran his tongue up and down the shaft, wrapping his lips around it and taking in as much as he could.

"Your lack of hair won't save you," the demon whispered, grabbing fistfuls of black curls and forcing Demetrius down to the base. "This is what you were made for."

Demetrius choked and drooled around the thick cock, struggling to breathe. The demon was ruthless, thrusting relentlessly until Demetrius' throat was raw and his lips chapped and bleeding.

With a final thrust, the priest forced himself into Demetrius until his nose was buried in the tight blond curls. The man of God held him there, shaking and choking, stretching Demetrius' throat and blocking his airway. Just as the light began to fade from his eyes, the demon pulled out and dropped him while Demetrius heaved and gasped, dragging air into hungry lungs.

Without ceremony, the demon positioned himself behind Demetrius and thrust into him, giving the exhausted and air-deprived man no time to react or adjust. The priest set a steady rhythm, pumping in and out and slapping Demetrius' ass. Demetrius curled his toes and grit his teeth, trying to relax and take in the strap-on. The priest shifted and Demetrius was hit with a sudden wave of pleasure.

"Therefore, submit to God," the priest recited. "Resist the devil and he will flee from you." He continued to push into Demetrius, building the pleasure before reaching down and rubbing the neglected, swollen clitoris. "But you've been running your whole life, Demetrius. Maybe that makes you the true devil."

Demetrius couldn't argue even if he wanted to. He knew what he was, in his soul. A black hole. A darkness. A penetrative, ebbing pain. But he couldn't think about that right now, not with a priest fucking him senseless, dragging him closer and closer to climax.

Around him, the lights on the church ceiling lit up one by one, shining down onto pews that were no longer empty. Naked and fucked, Demetrius made eye contact with people from his past. First, the old priest of his church who had threatened him with hellfire. Then the boy that his parents had pushed him into courtship with, followed by the various church members who had tried to persuade Demetrius to turn back onto the path of God. And finally, his parents, in the very front row. A cold chill overcame his entire body and for a moment, the world seemed fuzzy and distant, a hazy ripple that framed both his parents. Demetrius wanted to look away but he couldn't. He tried to focus, to blink them away but each time he was distracted by a pointed thrust that took his breath away and left him moaning.

The priest did not slow down, slapping Demetrius' ass, fucking him to the point of breaking, laughing gleefully with each new face in the crowd. Demetrius was red with shame, but too far gone to care about anything other than the release the devil was denying him. He tried not to look toward the disapproving faces in the crowd, focusing instead on the floor. That is until the priest pushed in extra hard, jolting Demetrius' head up. He realized that the crowd gazed without really seeing. Demetrius looked into his mother's familiar dead inside doe-eyes but they didn't look back. Instead, they seemed to look past him, frozen on some place or person beyond him. In fact, as he flicked his sight from one pair of eyes to another, he realized no one truly saw him. It wasn't surprising, really. It's what they had done his whole life. And even now, fucked raw by a priest, no one intervened on his behalf, no one gasped or looked away, no one reacted in the slightest. To Demetrius, what they did was worse. They stared at him with the same pitying, borderline disgusted look he had seen every Sunday.

The priest leaned forward, using his one free hand to snake through Demetrius' curls. "Submit," he hissed, pulling Demetrius' hair, lifting his head up.

With a final cry of shame, Demetrius submitted and came, staining the floor of the church, spilling all over the priest's hands. The waves of pleasure rolled through him as he rocked himself on the priest's cock, nursing his orgasm as long as it could last. The orgasm turned into multiple, and Demetrius came again and again, shaking to the point he thought he would break. He opened his eyes as the last powerful wave went through him and just as he peaked, the light came on in the very back of the church, shining down on a crucifix. Demetrius cried as the wave washed through him, his eyes fixating onto the body of Christ nailed to the weathered cross. Except it wasn't really Jesus. Demetrius recognized the curve of perfectly smooth alabaster hip bones, the soft brown birthmark kissing the left lower rib, sepia freckles dotting the skin like starlight constellations. He refused to believe what he saw, blinking and shaking his head. It couldn't be–

Demetrius' vision cleared as he locked eyes with his beloved Jupiter, the only person who had ever fully seen him and who now stared him down, bleeding and weeping in pain. Demetrius froze in shock, embarrassment, and fear. He was overcome with remorse and betrayal, a Judas to his sacrificial Christ.

The priest pulled out of Demetrius in one swift, brutal motion, pushing Demetrius forward until he collapsed on the stage. Every muscle in his body was screaming and all he could do was sit in the wet spot of his sin and quietly weep. He tried to crawl towards his lover, but his legs could not carry him. He reached an arm towards the cross, dragging himself down the stage steps, worn carpet scraping against his skin.

Demetrius had always looked at Jupiter as though he were God and now, he hung on the cross just like one. Blood dripped down from the nails embedded through Jupiter's wrists and feet. His arms were bound to the cross with rope, a simple cloth covering his groin, and on his head a crown of thorns that dug into his skin, rendering bloody rivers streaming down his face. He breathed erratically, painfully, his chest rising and falling in pained labor. Weakly, he raised his head until his eyes met Demetrius.

"Demetrius, my love," he whispered, "why did you abandon me?" He choked on the last word, erupting into terrible gasping, more blood leaking out of his lips.

The priest, garbed in his black robes once again, walked down the aisle motioning the crowd to turn their eyes to the cross.

"Cast all your cares on him," he said, turning to face Demetrius, "for he truly does suffer for you."

"Demetrius," Jupiter moaned.

Demetrius continued dragging himself down the aisle way as the seated flock observed his struggle. His tears fell freely, his agony inconceivable. His heart wrenched in a thousand ways and he couldn't comprehend how his beloved had ended up on a cross. His joints cracked and popped, his skin ripped open and bled, bruises of every color blotted his entire body. But to Demetrius, there was no pain quite like the anguish of seeing Jupiter hanging there, bloody and broken. He had felt plenty of heartbreak in his life but nothing had even come close to this. The priest watched silently; a smug smile etched into his face. He waited for Demetrius to reach the cross.

When Demetrius finally reached Jupiter, he collapsed brokenly before the cross. His skin was on fire as he mustered the last of his strength to raise himself to his knees. He sat back on his heels, prone and bare before his crucified Christ.

"But when they came to Jesus and found that he was already dead, they did not break his legs." The priest spoke again, drawing from his robe a glinting silver dagger. "Instead, one of the soldiers pierced Jesus' side with a spear, bringing a sudden flow of blood and water." He flicked his wrist, extending his arm, slicing across Jupiter's abdomen, erupting a brutal, agonizing scream from the golden-haired man.

"No!" Demetrius let out a blood curdling scream. "No, please, let him go. You can have me, I am enough. Please, please let him go!"

The priest smiled as he twisted the blade inside Jupiter before wrenching it away in a brutal pull. Demetrius flinched as the spouting blood painted his face and body, bathed in the blood of his beloved. He reached for Jupiter's mangled feet and cradled them against his face, weeping bitterly.

"No water. Only blood," the priest observed, rubbing the sticky fluid between his forefinger and thumb. "I guess your God is just a human after all." He plunged his hand into the gaping wound, pushing aside organs and intestines until he found his prize. Gripping firmly, he tore out Jupiter's uterus, holding it as it pulsated. Demetrius had never seen a uterus in the flesh, had never wanted to. The priest held it before him, the ovaries and tubes hanging like wilted vines. He raised it to his face, inhaling deeply before dragging his tongue across the marbled surface.

"Rejected inheritances from the Lord are best consumed fresh."

Without ceremony, the demon bared his ugly black teeth, ripping into the crimson organ. It squeaked between them, rubbery and textured. Demetrius hated the sound of it and begged the priest to stop.

"Please," he weeped brokenly still clinging to Jupiter, "Please let him go. You have taken enough. He didn't deserve this. Please, I'll do anything."

The salivating entity could not be deterred, however, and he continued to suckle and slurp until the dripping uterus disappeared down his throat and into his belly.

"Now, now," the priest answered, cracking his neck and stretching his back, "I really don't think you have much more to give. I think I've taken just about everything. Tell me, was I as good as Jupiter? Did I fill you with the Holy Ghost?"

"Fuck you!" Demetrius screamed, slipping in the blood that continued to pour from the ugly wound. Demetrius cried as he haphazardly pushed back the other organs that were now spilling out. He pressed them gently as Jupiter continued to cry and moan, before scooping up handfuls of the red liquid and pouring it back into Jupiter.

"Please," Demetrius whispered, "I need you to be okay. I need you to be okay. I need you. I need you I need you I need you."

The light that seemed to endlessly glow around Jupiter began to fade. His skin took on a sickly pallor, his handsome face wracked in grief and pain and confusion. Demetrius looked on and saw his boyfriend, possibly for the first time, not as golden god but as a human boy ravaged by an unforgiving cross.

"Jupiter," Demetrius cried, clinging desperately to the cross. "I love you. I'm so sorry. I'm so sorry."

Jupiter sputtered, a strangled breath easing from his lungs, carrying his final words, "I forgive you. You could not help it, for all that has been done to you."

Demetrius sobbed, his sorrow wracking his battered frame. He sobbed for the child that had never been properly loved, for the teenager who had not been accepted, and for the lover who had begun to heal him only to be cast out. His eyes poured forth saltwater tears that softened the stained rivulets of blood and his chest heaved as he felt the infernal suffering of what it was to love a God.

"Come now, Demetrius," the priest spoke again. "You act like you haven't had fun, like all you've experienced is upset. That seems very ungrateful of you. Perhaps you need to be taught again." With a firm hand, he grabbed Demetrius' curls again, attempting to pull him from the cross and back down the aisle.

Demetrius screamed, clinging to Jupiter, refusing to let go. He had let go before. He wouldn't this time. He wrapped his arms and legs around the cross, washing Jupiter's feet with his tears. He was so tired and so worn, but he dug deep into himself and pulled out the anger and sorrow that had been buried for a lifetime. It bolstered him and he yanked himself free, using the cross to pull himself up before finally letting go.

He stood before it, his tears all cried out. He'd spent his life running from its shadow. He'd tried to untangle himself from God and religion and all he had done was replace the body on the cross. Nobody was coming to save Demetrius, not the way he truly needed. He blinked and looked up and saw not Jupiter on the cross but himself. The thorns nestled into his curls, the gaping wound into his own abdomen. Nobody was coming to save Demetrius because his savior was already here. He had been here all along, in band tees and black jeans and shorn hair. The only person who had shown up for Demetrius time after time, even when Demetrius felt it wasn't enough.

Demetrius closed his eyes and when he opened them, he turned his head to see his arm outstretched, tied to the arm of the cross, a rusted iron nail plunged through his wrist. A clanging hammer interrupted him, and he looked to the other side, watching as he drove a second nail through his other wrist. He looked down and saw his parents push a third one into the thin, tender flesh of his feet. He watched as his father raised the hammer, smashing it down cruelly while his mother steadied the nail. His father looked up at him, hatred and disgust glowing in his eyes. His mother looked away, avoiding eye contact as she always had. He expected to cry but Demetrius had felt enough pain. He had suffered enough. He was tired of being crucified.

Demetrius inhaled deeply and with an excruciating cry, he ripped an arm free from the cross, tendons snapping and veins spraying, the stub of his arm holding his severed hand by a strip of flesh. His entire body was on fire, the pain receptors in his brain struggling to comprehend and keep up with the trauma. Every breath felt like it was his last. Every movement as if he was being torn apart and fed to dogs and demons. He repeated, freeing his second arm, wrapping his bloody stumps under his legs as he ripped them free, too. He fell from the cross, a pile of shredded muscles and splintered bones, broken teeth cutting his tongue. In the midst of his suffering, Demetrius felt a lightness. A freeness. He laid down, feeling the life flow out of him as a heaviness crept into his eyes. Perhaps he'd sleep now, a real sleep.

In the distance, Demetrius heard a chiming melody. As he slipped away, he wondered if it was the trumpets of the angels, if the end had come and he'd wake to the fire of which he'd been taught.

“Excuse me, sir, I think you need to wake up!” an urgent voice paired with equally urgent hands shook Demetrius from his slumber.

Demetrius shot up, blinking and gasping for air inside the airplane chapel. He was still there, and his legs had fallen asleep. He looked over to the person shaking him and it was a priest. Demetrius jerked back as if burned, falling out the chair and pulling himself up and away. He didn't turn his back on the priest or the open doors. Not this time.

“I'm so sorry to bother you, but your alarm was going off, and I was afraid you weren't going to wake up!”

Demetrius realized this priest was different. He was not the one from earlier or the one from his dreams. This one was young, his outfit a bit disheveled, nervousness peeking in brown eyes framed by rectangular glasses.

Demetrius pulled himself together and checked his phone, which was still screaming at him. He silenced the alarm and turned back to the priest. "Thank you for waking me, I guess I was a bit stuck in my slumber."

"It happens," the priest chuckled, stepping back as Demetrius lurched in front of the chair on unstable feet.

"Do you need any help?" the man of God queried.

Demetrius raised an eyebrow before shaking his head. "No, I'm just gonna catch my plane and go home."

"Godspeed," answered the priest. "Have a safe flight."

Demetrius opened his phone again, the time checking just past 9:15pm. He was grateful the priest had awakened him. He didn't have time to process everything that had happened...that he had dreamed? He was just happy to be alive and not mounted on a cross or crying over a bleeding boyfriend.

Boyfriend.

Demetrius stopped midstride, pulling up Jupiter's chat bubble.

> Hey. I honestly don't know what to say to you except that I am so sorry. I was a total asshole and if you never wanted to speak to me again I would understand. I have a lot to sort out

> but I would love the chance to do it with you.
>   To let you be part of it.
>   If you'll have me?

Demetrius hit send and waited for what felt like an eternity, checking his phone repeatedly as he continued the walk to his final terminal. As he rounded the corner towards his gate, a reply lit up his phone.

> I didn't reach out first only because
> I didn't want to upset you more on
> your flight. Are you home? Call me.

> I love you.

Demetrius blinked back tears as he sent a quick reply that he would be home soon, and he could call. The lump that had formed in his throat disintegrated and his steps grew lighter. A million thoughts and feelings swirled in his head. What was real? What was a dream? He was convinced he'd had a run in with the devil– though he felt it was one of his own making rather than one from the bible. A feeling of dread returned when he began thinking about how he would tell Julie or Jupiter about his encounter. Would they believe him? He wasn't sure he believed himself. The only thing he knew with certainty was that he had to get the fuck out of this airport.

He approached the ticket scanner, double checking that the flight was on time and ready to go.

"We are all set, just have a seat and come up when your group is called," the associate said, puzzled by Demetrius' giddy excitement over the plane's departure.

Demetrius settled into a chair, overcome with relief that his nightmare was almost over. He texted his sister the update.

> About to board. Be home soon.

About fucking time. Don't crash <3

Demetrius rubbed his arms, wincing as his hands touched a wrist. On either side was an ugly purple and blue bruise, made more gruesome by the swollen green veins. He started, a panic creeping into his chest. He looked around him. There were no priests or demons or crosses. Just other tired travelers, suitcases, and neck pillows. Demetrius couldn't completely understand everything he had experienced. He'd heard stories about deconstructionists experiencing a crisis of faith before they fully split, but it had never been as gruesome or brutal as this. Or, he reasoned, maybe there are things we just always keep locked away.

A sermon from his past life also ate away at his brain. The one about demons and possessions and temptations. Demetrius shook it away. He didn't believe in that anymore. Did he? He wondered if he would always be this conflicted, if the shadow of the cross would ever cast itself over anything but him. Demetrius found himself at a loss for answers.

But he did have Jupiter. And Julie. And himself. Maybe that would be enough.

Demetrius rose tiredly one more time as his group number was called. He stood in line for only a moment before making his way to the front. He scanned his ticket, walked down the aisle way and found the way to his seat. He took a quick peak around and saw towards the back of the plane, the young, nervous priest. The priest smiled at Demetrius, black pointed teeth peeking through full lips before he was cut off by a suitcase being loaded into the compartments. When Demetrius' vision cleared, the teeth were gone, and it was only the rumpled priest quietly reading his Bible. The cold sweat and heart palpitations began anew, the aching trauma returning from his last encounter. Demetrius was taking no chances and he stumbled forward to confront the priest.

"What are you doing on this flight? Are you following me?!"

The priest looked up, frightened. "I'm so sorry it was just a coincidence I promise. I'm just going home to my family."

A flight attendant rushed over, threatening to remove Demetrius.

"No, no it's not necessary. It was a misunderstanding," the priest assured her. "I'll pray for you," he directed to Demetrius.

Demetrius ignored the priest and looked around. He was surrounded by haggard and disgruntled passengers, cumbersome luggage, and wary stewards. He apologized to the flight attendant and made his way back to his seat. He checked his phone and saw the time was now just past midnight.

"We're now preparing for take off please direct your attention to the attendants in the row, thank you." The pilot's voice rang out over the fuzzy intercom.

Demetrius took his seat, buckled his belt, and took a deep breath. He placed a hand over his erratic heart and calmed himself by repeating in his head all the safety instructions. He looked for the life raft under his chair, for the nearest exit, and of course for the nearest bathroom.

As the flight attendants made their way to their own seats, the cabin lights dimmed and Demetrius leaned back in his chair, exhausted. He was thankful it was a short flight–he'd be home within two hours and Julie would be there waiting for him. He tried not to fall asleep to the rumbling vibrations as the airplane wheels departed from the tarmac.

About the Author

M.C. Crane is a shapeshifter who resides in the 'Bermuda Triangle' of the United States where they dodge cryptids, conjure gay frogs, and only succumb to the Bible Belt when it's in the bedroom. Made of cosmic nonbinary stardust, they spend most of their time writing religious horror and surviving out of spite. Terminal Inferno (The Laughing Man House) is their first novella and the beginning of unfathomable horrors.